Big Trouble
in Little Twinsville

Also by Elizabeth Levy

KEEP MS. SUGARMAN IN THE FOURTH GRADE

MY LIFE AS A FIFTH-GRADE COMEDIAN

SCHOOL SPIRIT SABOTAGE

SAM AND ROBERT BAMFORD BOOKS

DRACULA IS A PAIN IN THE NECK

FRANKENSTEIN MOVED IN ON THE FOURTH FLOOR

BIG TROUBLE
in Little Twinsville

Elizabeth Levy

ILLUSTRATED BY
Mark Elliott

HARPERCOLLINS*PUBLISHERS*

To Erica and Dana, close enough to
be twins and twins in my heart.
Special thanks to Susan Chang for
making this book so much better.

Library of Congress Cataloging-in-Publication Data
Levy, Elizabeth.
  Big trouble in little Twinsville / Elizabeth Levy ; illustrated by Mark
Elliott.
     p.   cm.
  Summary: Sometimes Eve feels overwhelmed by her two younger twin
sisters, but things really get out of hand when the family decides to attend
a festival for twins at the Twinsville resort.
  ISBN 0-06-028590-7 — ISBN 0-06-028591-5 (lib. bdg.)
     [1. Twins—Fiction.   2. Sisters—Fiction.]   I. Elliott, Mark, ill.
II. Title.
PZ7.L5827 Bi 2001   00-059701
[Fic]—dc21   CIP
                                                                  AC

Typography by Andrea Simkowski
1 3 5 7 9 10 8 6 4 2
❖
First Edition
Visit us on the World Wide Web!
www.harperchildrens.com

CONTENTS

I

BIG MISTAKE

Twin terrors trespass!

Amy and May, the twin terrors, were in my room again.

"Get out," I said. "I have to clean my room before we go to the beach."

They ignored me as usual.

Amy grabbed one of my dinosaur models. Her fingers were sticky with peanut butter. May reached for my deinoychus model, pound-for-pound one of the fiercest dinosaurs of them all. Just like my twin sisters.

"Go wash your hands!" I rescued my stegosaurus from Amy and put it back on the shelf, with its claws facing left. I put all my plant-eating dinosaurs with their claws facing left, and the meat-eaters, like T-rex and deinoychus, with their claws facing right. They like it that way and so do I.

May jumped on my bed and started bouncing up and down. Pillows went flying. My very favorite royal blue comforter with gold suns and moons had dirty footprints all over it.

"Oh, no, May, I just made my bed!" I grabbed for her, but she just bounced away. She's a slippery little thing. Before I could get her off, Amy was bouncing on the bed too.

"You can't make us leave, Eve Peeve!" Amy chanted. Amy has the most horrible singsong voice in the world. Then May chimed in, "Eve Peeve, can't make us leave. Eve Peeve, can't make us leave." May has an equally horrible high-pitched squeak. Together they sound like yodeling chipmunks. Unfortunately, they are so used to singing to each other that they think they're terrific.

I couldn't stand it. Sticky peanut butter all over my room, footprints on my favorite comforter, a squawking horrible song about

me. I couldn't believe that I had asked for a baby sister or brother. I was an innocent five-year-old back then. And when Mom and Dad found out they were having twins, I was actually excited about the idea. Especially since I helped name them.

Dad and I came up with the names when we were playing a word game on the computer. "Amy" and "May" have the same letters in them. I noticed it first. My parents didn't want to give the twins rhyming names, so they thought "Amy" and "May" were perfect. I did, too.

I love playing with letters. You can say *my* name backward and forward and it's always spelled the same. My name is Eve. Eve was the first woman on earth. I was born first in my family. I think that's neat. But Eve never had any little sisters. Lucky for her. All she had to worry about was *one* snake in the garden of Eden. I have to worry about two. You can't tell them apart. And you can't get rid of them.

"Eve Peeve!" shouted Amy. "Eve Peever!" added May. She was born three minutes later, but she's just as noisy. They were both still jumping on my bed and squawking.

I had to get them out of my room. Then I had a brilliant idea. I have a Three Stooges screensaver on my computer that shows the Sultans of Slapstick throwing pies at each other. My dad and I both love the Three Stooges. He gave me Curly, Moe, and Larry action figure dolls for my last birthday. They are collector's items. They live in a special locked box next to my doll house. I hide the key under the hooked rug my aunt Norma made for my dollhouse, so the terrible two-some can't get their sticky hands on them.

The twins got off the bed and stood next to me. First, I made a banner that looked like it was coming out of the Three Stooges' mouths. Then I typed some words on the banner. Next, I printed it out in big letters, the biggest my computer would allow. I neatly taped the pieces together. When it was all done, it looked like Larry, Moe, and Curly were saying,

ONLY ONE VISITOR ALLOWED AT A TIME!

NO EXCEPTIONS!

THIS MEANS YOU!

I hung the banner over the door. Amy and May looked at it. They looked at each other. They tried to sound out the letters, but they can't read well yet. I pointed to each word very slowly, and read it to them out loud.

"From now on, only one of you can be in my room at a time. A rule's a rule," I said in a sweet voice. I knew them. Neither would want to be the one who had to leave. And nobody could say I was kicking them out.

Amy and May looked at each other for a split second. Then, without saying a word, they decided what to do. They both screamed at the exact same second. It drives me nuts that they can do that. Somehow they manage to scream at different pitches. I put my fingers in my ears.

My father came running up to my room. "What's wrong?"

The twins grabbed for his legs and hung on him. I used to hang on my dad's leg too, but when I did it, at least he had one leg free. The putrid pair kept screeching their heads off, acting like I had done something awful to them. All I had done was put up a sign.

"A lot's going on, Dad," I said. "Amy and

May bounced all over my bed. They—"

Dad interrupted me. "I mean why are the twins screaming?"

"Because they're a screaming machine," I muttered.

Dad put his hands on the twins' heads. "What's wrong?"

Amy pointed to my sign. "Eve's mean," she whined.

Then May started in. "Mean Eve Peeve," she sobbed.

I couldn't believe it—she had managed to make herself cry! I don't know how she did it. I hadn't even touched her.

"Dad," I protested. "Look what they did to my poor bed."

The gruesome twosome started giggling as if they were proud of the mess they had made. They can go from giggles to tears and back again faster than Curly can throw a whipped cream pie at Moe. Then they bolted out of the room.

I picked up the pillows from the floor and started to remake my bed. Dad came and helped me. "Uh, Eve," he said.

I looked up. "Dad, no good sentence in

my life ever started 'Uh . . . Eve. . . .'"

Dad glanced at my banner. "Well, about your new rule . . ." He pointed to the sign on my door. "I'm not sure it's fair."

"It's very fair," I said. "After all, I didn't say *Amy* and *May* keep out. That might have been unfair. I said one visitor at a time. It's a rule for everybody!"

"You'll make either a great lawyer or a great law-maker someday," said Dad. "Just like your mom."

I stared at him. I loved Mom and all, but I wasn't sure I wanted to be *just* like her. Mom's a lawyer. She had to go back to work when the twins were just six weeks old. Dad's an accountant. He works at home. So Dad and I basically took care of the twins when they were little. I was a *great* big sister when they were babies. But now they are almost five, the age I was when they were born, and it's a whole different ball game.

"It's a good rule," I insisted. "As good as your rule about Mom having to leave her phone when she goes to the beach." Mom never goes anywhere without a cell phone stuck to her ear. Dad and my aunt Norma challenged her to spend at least one day a weekend unplugged.

"Well, that's a great rule," said Dad. "But I think your rule may need a few kinks worked out. For example, if it's only one visitor at a time, what about when Mom and I come in together to kiss you good night?"

"You can come in one at a time. It's a sacrifice I'm willing to make."

"Eve, your sisters are younger than you are. They don't understand rules in the same way. You've got to be patient."

I never liked that word. Patient. That's what they called me last summer when I had to go to the hospital because I broke my foot. Correction—when the twins made me break my foot by tripping me and then landing right on top of me.

"Now, why don't you put on your bathing suit and get ready for the beach," Dad suggested, reacting to the face I was making.

"Maybe I'll just stay home with you," I said.

"Don't be silly," said Dad. "I have a lot of work to do. And Lindsay and Karen will be there. Besides, Mom will need your help getting the twins to the beach."

I sighed. "They're sooo much trouble."

Dad laughed. "Well, you're the one who wanted a baby sister," he said.

Dad keeps reminding me that I had begged my parents for a baby sister or brother.

Still, I didn't ask for two at once. Two was a very big mistake.

I only ordered one.

2

WHO ARE YOU CALLING A SIMPLETON?

My new bathing suit was blue with yellow sunflowers. I had a matching blue straw hat with a sunflower on it and blue sandals with a sunflower between my big toe and my second toe.

My grandma bought me the entire outfit. She knows I like to plan outfits that match. I looked at myself in the mirror. I liked what I saw. I was the sunflower kid. Blue is my best color. I like sky blue, deep blue, sapphire, and turquoise. True blue means that you're loyal, and I'm loyal to the color blue.

Amy and May don't know how to be loyal to a color. Now that the twins are old enough, they are sometimes allowed to pick out their own clothes. The results are horrible. They should be called the "clash twins." They've never met a color they didn't like and they usually try to wear them all at once.

I took one last look at myself in the mirror. Then I went downstairs to the kitchen. It was my job to pack the picnic basket. I'm a very good packer. I know exactly how to save space. I put in little tubes of peanut butter and jelly—they're so much easier than the big jars at picnics. I put in fruit and salami. I love salami. I made sure there were plenty of napkins.

Mom came in to check everything. "Sweetie, you did a great job. Now let me put some sunblock on you before we leave. But we've got to hurry."

As usual, Mom couldn't remember where she had put the tube of sunblock. She was still looking when the twins came running into the kitchen, almost bowling me over.

"MOM!" I couldn't believe what I was seeing.

"What's wrong?" She finally looked up.

"Look at what they're wearing!" May and Amy were dressed exactly like me. They had on blue bathing suits with yellow sun-flowers, identical blue straw hats with a sun-flower on them, and sunflower sandals.

Amy started skipping around me, chanting. "Eve looks like us!"

"We look like Eve!" giggled May.

"Mom, get them out of those suits," I insisted. "Grandma sent me this outfit for my birthday and I'm sure she didn't want you to go out and buy the exact same thing for the twins."

"We asked her!" shrieked Amy.

"What!" I turned to Mom. "How could you?"

Mom sighed. "Amy and May *did* ask your grandmother if they could have a suit just like yours. You know we don't usually dress the twins alike. But they begged and begged . . . and they do look cute."

I stared at the twins. They looked so adorable in their outfits—correction, *my* outfit—with their long red hair and round blue eyes, that it made me sick to my stomach. I glared at Mom. "I'm going upstairs to change!"

"Eve, we don't have time. Please, don't make a fuss about this. The twins look up to you. You're their big sister and they just want to be like you. You're not usually selfish, so let's give this one a rest. You look adorable in that outfit too. We'll just go to the beach right now."

When Mom used that tone, I knew arguing wouldn't do any good. I grabbed the picnic basket and stomped off to the car. The twins skipped after me.

"Eve is selfish," chirped Amy.

"Eve is a shellfish!" May repeated.

I gritted my teeth and tried to ignore them. I did not like being called selfish or a shellfish. This was not going to be a good day at the beach. I could tell already.

When we got to the beach, we had to park a long way from the water. Mom put on a huge knapsack with all the beach towels in it. She turned to me and said, "Eve, if you take the umbrella and picnic basket, I can hold the twins' hands. I don't want them running in the parking lot."

The umbrella was huge. It was heavy and really hard to carry. How was I going to carry the basket too? Then I figured it out. I put the umbrella over my shoulder and stuck the picnic basket over the pointed end.

Mom looked at me and laughed. "Oh dear," she said. "You look like a donkey that has too much to carry."

"Great," I said. "I'm a donkey disguised as a sunflower."

"Donkey, donkey!" shouted Amy.

"Donkey, monkey!" May blurted out. She grinned as if she had just made up the most brilliant rhyme in the world.

"Thanks, Mom. You *would* have to call me a donkey," I muttered.

"You're a very cute donkey," said Mom. "Come on, let's go." She took hold of the twins' hands and started off.

"It's too hot," whined May.

"Mommy, carry me!" begged Amy.

"No, sweetie. You're too big to be carried," said Mom.

Amy stuck out her lower lip. Then she walked right on top of a half-empty McDonald's bag that some slob had thrown on the ground. Ketchup and mustard squirted out of the bag and splattered all over her legs. Amy wiped her legs and got ready to lick her fingers.

"Yuck! Don't lick your fingers!" I shouted. "Wipe them off on something."

Amy wiped her fingers on my legs.

"Not on me!" I wailed.

"Eve, what's the problem?" asked Mom, turning around.

"Amy just got garbage all over me."

"I'm sticky," said Amy. "I can't carry all this." She dropped her inflatable alligator.

"Neither can I," whined May. Her turtle joined Amy's alligator.

"Eve, can you please help them out?" Mom asked. "Otherwise it'll take us forever to get out of the parking lot."

I put down the picnic basket and umbrella. "Mom. You already told me I look like a donkey."

Mom smiled at me. "Well, what else does a donkey need but an alligator? And maybe a turtle." She took off my hat and put the alligator around one shoulder, and the turtle around the other. Then she put my sunflower hat back on my head. Now all the twins were carrying were their teeny-tiny beach pails.

"Great!" I muttered. "Scientists will probably think I'm a new species—one-fourth sunflower, one-fourth alligator, one-fourth donkey, and one-fourth turtle."

Mom laughed. "You do look like something the Museum of Natural History would like to study."

Amy and May danced around me singing, "Donkey toes . . . alligator teeth . . . turtle neck . . ." Naturally, they sang off-key. They skipped ahead and took Mom's hands.

I tried to walk forward. The wind picked up underneath the umbrella and sent me scooting backward. Then the wind shifted and I staggered to the left. It shifted to the right, and I stumbled right.

"Do you need help?" asked a woman behind me.

"Yes, please." I looked up thankfully.

But the woman completely ignored me and charged right up to the twins. She took the teeny-tiny buckets from them. "What adorable little darlings you are. I just love your sunflower bathing suits," she gushed.

When she saw me, she did a double take.

"You're all dressed alike! I get it. I bet you wish you were a twin too, or that you were all triplets. You must be the big sister."

People say the dumbest things when they see twins. For example, thinking that even in my wildest dreams—or nightmares, more like it—I would ever, ever, *ever* want to be a twin or triplet with Amy and May.

Mom laughed. "You've got it right. Eve's the big sister."

"We're four," said Amy. She stuck four grubby fingers in the air.

"Four score!" said May.

The woman laughed. I don't know where May had picked that up.

"You are both so smart and cute," said the woman in that icky voice that adults sometimes use. She looked down at me. "You're a very lucky girl to have such adorable sisters."

Now, I ask you. I'm standing in front of her carrying an umbrella with a picnic basket balanced over the end, an alligator inner tube around one shoulder, and a turtle around the

other. And she thinks I'm lucky.

A gust of wind caught at the umbrella again. I tried to control it, but I got twirled around. The picnic basket fell off the end of the umbrella. It dropped on the woman's foot, and she kind of staggered a little. Then she fell right on her butt.

"Eve!" said Mom, sounding alarmed. The twins went to the lady and tried to help her up. I knew they were doing it just because I was in trouble.

"Oh, thank you, darlings. You are so sweet." She glared at me.

"Sorry," I said. "This stuff's heavy."

"Eve's peeved!" chirped Amy.

"Eve's sneezed!" chimed in May.

The woman laughed. "Aren't they just cuter than cute? You *must* take these honeys to the twin festival in Twinsville."

"I've heard about the festival," said Mom.

"My name is Dorothy Keller. I'm the director of the festival and the mother of twin boys. *Double the trouble, double the fun,* I always say. My little boys are all grown up now. They live far away and can't come this year."

She sniffed and got all teary-eyed. "My boys and I went to the festival every year and always had such fun. I used to dress them up in the most precious little trouser suits with matching bow ties. They just *loved* it."

I stared at her. I bet her boys couldn't wait to get out of having to go to the festival.

Mrs. Keller grabbed Mom's arm. "Do come to the festival. It's just for a weekend. It's held in the lovely Twin Falls Resort, which has a golf course and a beautiful swimming pool. We have all sorts of games, activities, and talent contests for the kids."

"A twin festival," I said under my breath. "What a nightmare."

I guess I must have said it louder than I meant to. Mrs. Keller looked down at me disapprovingly.

"My dear," she said. "I'm sure being a singleton isn't easy, but many singletons have fun at the festival."

"Simpletons—who are you calling a simpleton?" I wanted to take my umbrella and swing it at her again. "Lady, you don't know me. I'm very smart. I happen to have been the chess champion of the third grade."

"A *singleton*, not a simpleton, my dear. A singleton is anyone who is not a twin, triplet, quadruplet—"

"Then all power to the singletons!" I said.

"All power to twins!" shrieked Amy and May.

"You know," said Mrs. Keller. "I think these little darlings would be the hit of the festival. You just have to take them." She and Mom exchanged business cards, and then she charged off.

"Mom! That lady was crazy. You always tell us not to talk to strangers. How come you let her go on so long?"

"Well, clearly she wasn't dangerous," said Mom. "And it's different. You were with me."

We got under way again. "You know, Eve," Mom mused. "Twin Falls Resort is supposed to be a very nice place for a vacation."

A vacation surrounded by twins? I couldn't imagine anything worse.

3

THE CRABS CRAWL IN, THE CRABS CRAWL OUT

"Hey, Eve, over here!" I heard my cousins calling and staggered in their direction. They ran over to help me. Lindsay took the picnic basket, and Karen took the umbrella. "Thank you, thank you," I said, slipping off my sandals.

I gawked at them. They gawked at me. We were all dressed in identical sunflower outfits. "Grandma!" we shrieked.

"Now I don't feel so bad," I said. "When I first saw the twins dressed like sunflowers, I wanted to plant them in the backyard headfirst."

"Speaking of the twins," said Lindsay,

"where are Tweedle Dum and Tweedle Dumber?"

Lindsay's just my age, ten, and Karen's nine. We've played together all our lives. Like me, they can remember a time when our family was just us—three cousins, all friends—and no twins!

I giggled. If I ever called the twins Tweedle Dum and Tweedle Dumber, I'd be in big trouble. "They'll be here in a minute—they're probably making Mom carry them."

I went over to say hi to my aunt Norma. She's Lindsay and Karen's mom, and my favorite aunt. She's the only one other than my father and me who likes pizza with anchovies. Everybody else holds their nose when we eat it. And she's just about the only one in the family who doesn't make the world's biggest fuss over the twins.

"What's new, pussycat?" she asked, giving me a hug. "Great outfit! Where's your mom and the twins? Are they sunflowers too? Oh, there they are now." Sometimes Aunt Norma talks a lot without stopping for a breath.

She jumped up to help Mom.

The twins dropped their pails on the beach blanket. They took each other's hands and started twirling around. "London twins are falling down!" they shouted in their awful singing voices.

Lindsay and Karen put their fingers in their ears.

"Can we go into the water?" asked Lindsay.

"Go on, kids," said Mom. "Norma and I will watch you from here."

I started to put my sandals back on. I hate to get sand on my feet.

Lindsay jumped up and started running. "Come on. Last one in is a rotten egg."

"Eve is too clean to be a rotten egg," teased Karen. She started running, too.

I finally got my sandals on and started to run after Lindsay and Karen.

Amy grabbed my hand. "Wait for us!" she shrieked.

May grabbed my other hand. "We want to go too!"

"Let go," I said, trying to shake them off. "You're making me lose."

Aunt Norma saw my predicament. "Come on, Amy and May. I'll go down to the water with you. We'll make a sand castle by letting the sand drip through our fingers." She took the twins off my hands.

Freed at last, I took off down the beach. I streaked past Karen, and then past Lindsay. I knew the sand was hot and must be burning their feet. So I could run faster. Sometimes taking a little bit of care right before doing something—like putting on your sandals—helps you in the long run.

I kicked off my sandals and jumped into the water. "I won!" I shouted. "I'm not a rotten egg!" The water was cold.

Lindsay and Karen jumped in, splashing me. They immediately stuck their heads under the water.

Lindsay popped up first. "I can't believe you won, Eve. I thought for sure we'd beat you when you stopped to put your sandals on."

I tiptoed out to her so the water got to my armpits. "Believe it," I said. "I like to win."

"Tell us something new," said Karen. "That's why I won't play chess with you. You always win."

"But you're good players too," I said.

Lindsay splashed water on me. "You

worry too much. Winning's fun! You're supposed to enjoy it."

"Hey, your mom's calling you," said Karen. I looked up.

"Eve," shouted Mom. "Come on out and let me put suntan lotion on you."

"I don't want to get out. I just got in." I tried to argue, but Mom gave me that look that said I'd better get out pronto. I told Lindsay and Karen that'd I'd be right back and waded out.

Amy and May were throwing clumps of sand at each other on the shore. Drip castles are supposed to be messy, but theirs were drooping messes. And they were covered with sand from head to foot.

"Hey, where are you going?" Amy asked.

"To put lotion on," I said.

"We come too!" shrieked May.

They ran after me and latched onto my leg. It felt like being grabbed by an octopus with sandpaper for tentacles.

"We put lotion on you," said Amy.

"No," I said. "Mom's going to do it. You two are full of sand."

"We want to do it," Amy whined.

"Mom!" shrieked May.

"What's wrong now?" asked Mom.

"Eve won't let us put suntan lotion on her. We just want to help. We do it good!" said Amy.

I rolled my eyes. "They'll get it all over my bathing suit and everything. And look at their hands. It'll be like getting rubbed by sandpaper."

"Eve, the twins are just trying to help," said Mom. "Amy and May, go to the water and wash your hands off. Then Eve will let you put lotion on her back."

I sighed. The twins *always* got their own way.

When the twins came back, I inspected their hands. Naturally, they were still grubby with sand. I took them back down to the water's edge to wash their hands again. Finally, I lay down and let the twins put the lotion on my back. The sooner it was over, the sooner I could go back in the water with Lindsay and Karen.

"Mom, did you get new lotion?" I asked. "It smells like peanuts."

"It's coconut," said Mom. "It's supposed to remind you of the Hawaiian Islands." She and Aunt Norma went back to their conversation. I could tell they were talking about the Twin Falls Resort. I didn't even want to think about it.

The sun felt warm on my back, and I began to relax. I had to admit the twins rubbing my back felt good. I guess sometimes two pairs of hands are better than one.

The twins stopped rubbing the lotion. Now I could feel their little tiny fingernails lightly scratching my back. "Ummm, that feels good," I said. They didn't answer. Sometimes the twins aren't all bad. Maybe I was too tough on them.

One of them, I couldn't tell who, began to lightly tickle my arm. I giggled. "That tickles." I wondered why I could feel so many little fingers on my back and on my legs. Even though they're twins, they only have twenty fingers between them, and it felt like a hundred fingers were tickling me up and down and all over. "That's enough," I said.

I opened one eye to see which one of them was doing it. Then I shrieked. I was looking straight at a sand crab. It was looking at me with its bulging eyes. Its little pinchers were clicking together. Its tiny feelers were quivering. So was I.

I scrambled to my feet and screamed. Sand crabs were crawling all over me! I could feel one in my hair. I jumped up and down. "Get them off me," I shrieked.

Lindsay and Karen came running and tried to brush them off me, but the sand crabs hung on. I could feel another one near my ear. "Mom! Help! I'm being attacked!"

"Eve is crabby!" Amy shrieked.

"Eve is a crabcake," May chanted.

"Eve is a shellfish!" yelled Amy.

"A shellfish selfish shellfish!" repeated May.

I couldn't believe they could laugh at me when I was being eaten alive in front of their eyes.

"Oh my goodness. Where did all these crabs come from?" said Mom.

"Mom," I said, fighting hard not to cry. "Get them off me."

"I'll get them off you." She took a towel and rubbed me with it. "There, I think they're all gone. Honest, honey . . . you're okay."

I was shaking. Mom hugged me. Then she wrinkled her nose like Samantha on *Bewitched*. "Why does your shoulder smell like peanut butter?" she asked.

"It's your new coconut suntan lotion," I said.

Mom ran her finger along my shoulder blade and then put her finger in her mouth. "Mom?" I said. "What are you doing?"

"It *is* peanut butter!" said Mom. "What are you doing with peanut butter on your shoulder?" She looked at my back. "It's all over you!"

"Two guesses!" I shouted.

The twins giggled and hid behind Mom. "We didn't do anything," whined Amy.

"Amy and May," said Mom. "What did you put on Eve's back? Let me see what you used."

The twins went to the picnic basket and pulled out a tube. Mom looked at the label. "Peanut butter," she said.

"They did it on purpose!" I sputtered.

The twins hid behind Mom again.

I grabbed the tube of peanut butter and shook it in their faces. "I could have ended up eaten to death by crabs."

"She could have gotten peanut butter in her nose and mouth and not been able to breathe," said Karen.

"She could have ended up as a crab cake with peanut butter sauce," said Lindsay.

The twins giggled.

"I'm glad you all think it's so funny," I said. "You didn't have sand crabs climbing all over you."

"Now, honey, it was an honest mistake," said Mom. "The twins can't read. And you were the one who picked out that peanut butter tube in the supermarket. Remember? You thought it was so much neater than a messy jar."

The twins smirked and stuck their tongues out at me.

"Come on," said Karen. "Let's go back in the water and you can get that gunk off you."

"Just be careful of peanut-butter-eating

sharks," said Aunt Norma.

Mom helped me put on the *real* sunscreen and then the three of us went back into the water. As I swam, I wondered if there really were sharks that liked peanut butter. Maybe I could put the rest of the tube on the twins.

4

LITTLE RABBIT FOU-FOU

On Sunday, Dad and I mowed the lawn together like we do every summer weekend. I sat next to Dad and gave him directions while he drove. We were making a checkerboard pattern in perfect squares. We get the pattern by making sure that the roller is extra heavy. Mom thinks we're crazy because it takes twice as long as mowing it normally, but Dad and I like it.

Karen and Lindsay and Aunt Norma rode up on their bikes. "I can't get over how neat your lawn looks—like a baseball diamond," said Aunt Norma. "That's my brother— the neatest man in the world. And Eve is a chip off the old block."

Dad stopped the mower and I got down. I liked being a chip off the old block if the old block was my dad. And I liked the idea of my lawn looking as beautiful as a diamond. I was happy that we had worked together and created something so beautiful.

"Hey, Eve," said Aunt Norma. "Careful in the sun. Are you sure you've got enough peanut butter on?"

"Very funny," I said.

Dad laughed. "I can see it's going to become a family legend: The Day the Twins Spread Peanut Butter All Over Eve."

I made a face. I wished there could be some family legends that didn't involve Amy and May.

Just then, Mom came out carrying her cell phone.

"Hey," shouted Aunt Norma. "I thought you swore off that thing during the weekends."

Mom smiled. "This wasn't a call about work. Eve, remember Mrs. Keller, the woman from the twin festival?"

"How could I forget her?" I said.

"Well, she just called and invited us to the festival. It's in two weeks at the Twin Falls Resort."

"Twin Falls?" said Dad. "That's supposed to have one of the best golf courses in the area. Why don't we go?"

"Well, I don't know. . . ." said Mom. "I've got a lot of work scheduled for that week."

For once, I was glad that she had a lot of work.

"Come on," said Dad. "It'll be a good break."

"I think it sounds like fun," said Karen. "Mom, can we go, too?"

"Does it have a swimming pool?" asked Lindsay.

"I'm sure it does," said Dad. "Why don't you kids go see if it has a website and report back. Tell us what you find out."

I could tell they wanted to talk about it by themselves. Lindsay, Karen, and I went up to my room and looked up Twinsville and the twin festival. At first glance, it was even worse than I thought. The town was founded by a pair of twins, Sadie and Madie. They married twin brothers named Abe and Gabe at a double wedding by the Twin Falls waterfalls. Later, the town became famous for the number of twins born there. I guess twin chlorine got into the town's gene pool.

"This is going to be a hoot," said Karen.

"It's going to be a twinmare," I said.

Lindsay was wandering around my room. She looked at the locked box with Curly, Moe, and Larry. "Can I touch them?" she asked.

"Sure," I said. Lindsay and Karen love the Three Stooges almost as much as I do. I took the key from under the rug and unlocked the box for her.

Karen and I went back to the computer. The resort looked nice—especially the huge swimming pool—but when we clicked on the links about the festival, there were way too many pictures of twins and triplets, and even quadruplets, for my taste.

Amy and May barged in. "What are you doing?"

"Out!" I pointed to my sign that was still up.

"Lindsay and Karen are in here!" said Amy. She put her hands on her hips. "One of them has to go, too!"

Lindsay giggled. "Amy's got your steel-trap kind of a mind. It's just the kind of thing you would say."

I sighed. They did have a point. I should have made a banner that said no identical-looking people in my room. I took down the banner and went back to my desk.

Amy pointed to the computer screen. "What's that?" she asked.

"It's about the twin festival in Twinsville," I said. "It's a place where everybody's just like you."

"Yeah," said Karen. "There's a talent show. And I bet there're lots of really, really talented twins."

May looked at Amy. I could see that didn't sound so good to them. They didn't say a word. Lindsay, Karen, and I went back to our research.

A little while later, we were interrupted by a horrible noise. *"Little Rabbit Fou-Fou, hopping through the forest . . . came upon a field mouse, bopped it on the head."* The twins were singing—correction, trying to sing—a song my dad had taught me and I had taught them.

"The good fairy came along and said, 'Little Rabbit Fou-Fou, stop bopping field mice, or I'll turn you into a goon!'"

Karen put her fingers in her ears. Lindsay and I can carry a tune, but Karen's got a great voice. It's actually painful for her when the twins try to sing. When our families get together for the holidays and sing carols, we always try to drown them out.

"Shut up!" we all shouted.

But nothing can stop the twins once they get started. They ran into their room and put on the rabbit ears that they had worn at Easter time. They hopped back into my room, singing the next verse with their ears flopping. They hopped onto my bed, making bopping motions with their fists.

Their singing was so loud and so off-key, it was torture. Unfortunately, the song has lots of verses. The good fairy gives Little Rabbit Fou-Fou three chances to stop bopping field mice on the head. When they got to the last verse, Amy reached into my box with the Three Stooges and grabbed Larry.

"Little Rabbit Fou-Fou," she sang, waving

him around by his legs.

"Hey!" I shouted. "Put him back."

May took out Moe and bopped Larry on the head with him.

I stepped in and grabbed both dolls from them. I held them over their heads.

"Nyuk, nyuk, nyuk. . . ." said Amy, trying to imitate the Three Stooges' laugh.

"New York, New York," echoed May, not sounding anything like Curly.

The twins giggled.

"It's not funny!" I said. That was the last straw. "You know you're not supposed to play with these dolls. They're very valuable." I locked the box again and put the key under the carpet and shoved the twins out the door.

"Sorry," said Lindsay. "I was the one who asked you to unlock the box."

"It's not your fault," I said. "It was the twins' fault. Life is so unfair. They get away with everything. I'd like to turn them into goons."

"I think the good fairy got there before you," said Karen. She finally took her fingers out of her ears.

We printed out the pages about the resort and took them back down to my parents and Aunt Norma. Dad was excited about the golf course. Aunt Norma loved the description of the four-star restaurants. Mom had the look of someone who was outvoted. "I guess it's Twin Falls—and the twin festival—here we come." She took out her electronic organizer. "I'll put it on my schedule."

5

Curly Loses His Head

Two weeks later, I was packing for our weekend at the Twin Falls Resort. I carefully folded my favorite Three Stooges T-shirt, the one with Curly, Moe, and Larry giving their famous "Nyuk, nyuk, nyuk" laugh. I was in a good mood. I know it sounds crazy to be looking forward to a weekend filled with twins, but Lindsay and Karen were coming, too. Mom promised no cell phone, no laptop, no work at all. And the twins had been strangely quiet lately. So all in all, I was feeling good.

Dad poked his head into my room. "Just wanted to check on your packing."

He looked at my suitcase. My hiking shoes were at the bottom where they wouldn't mess up my clothes. My bathing suit was tucked into my bathing cap—just in case the hotel made you wear one in the pool. And I had packed an extra suit so that while one was wet, I'd always have a dry one.

"Perfect," he said. "I wish you would give your mom packing lessons. Since you're all ready, could you do Mom and me a favor? Let the twins play in here for a few minutes while we finish packing and cleaning up the rest of the house."

I looked around my room. Then I closed my suitcase as a precaution. It looked pretty safe. "Okay," I said.

The twins bopped into my room.

"Sit down on my bed and don't touch anything," I told them.

They sat. They looked at the locked box that held Curly, Larry, and Moe. "Aren't you taking them?" asked Amy.

"Of course not," I said. "They're too good to take."

"Mom and Dad said that we could take two dolls each," said May.

"Curly, Moe, and Larry are action figures, not dolls," I explained.

"They don't get much action," piped up Amy.

I stared at her. Sometimes she sounds like she's four going on thirteen.

"I think you should take them," said May.

"Me, too," said Amy.

I thought about it. It might be fun to have them along. Lindsay and Karen know the Three Stooges routines almost as well as I do. We could play with them during all the boring twin activities. Then I thought better of it. The chance of their getting damaged was too big.

"No," I said.

"Let's play with them now," said Amy.

"Yeah!" said May.

"Absolutely not! Now sit there like I told you while I check my e-mail."

"Fou-fou fou, la, la, la," chirped Amy in a singsong voice.

"Fou-fou falafel . . ." added May.

I groaned. The twins were at it again— talking in their stupid "fou-fou" language.

I ignored them and opened up my e-mail. There was a very funny *bon voyage* greeting card from Lindsay, even though she was coming, too, and a long e-mail from another cousin in California. I got so involved in answering that e-mail that I almost forgot the twins were in the room.

I heard May sing, *"Little Rabbit Fou-Fou, hopping through the forest . . . came upon a field mouse, bopped it on the head."*

She sounded awful, but I have to admit I love the song. Without looking around, I chimed in. *"The good fairy came along and said, 'Little Rabbit Fou-Fou, stop bopping field mice, or I'll turn you into a . . .'"* When I got to the word "goon," I swiveled around.

My action figure box was open. Amy had Curly by his legs, and she was swinging him around. *"Little Rabbit Fou-Fou,"* she sang.

My eyes practically popped out of my head.

"Nyuk, nyuk, nyuk!" yelled May.

"Hey!" I shouted, lunging at Amy. "Put him back."

Amy flung Curly in May's direction. She caught him by the head. Then she dropped him on the wooden floor. Curly's head shattered into a million pieces.

I screamed my head off. The twins were

quiet, for once. May's mouth popped open. She looked frozen.

Mom and Dad came running into the room. "What is it? What's wrong, Eve?" Mom asked.

I couldn't speak. I pointed to the headless body on the floor.

Mom sank down on my bed. "I thought someone was murdered, the way you were screaming."

"It *was* murder!" I howled.

The twins cowered behind Dad.

"Eve, calm down," said Dad. He picked up the limp, headless body.

"Calm down!" I screeched. "How can I calm down? Dad, it's Curly. They broke into my locked box . . . they . . ."

"I'm sure it was an accident," said Mom.

"Accident! Breaking into my locked box! And I know it was locked. Just a couple of weeks ago, when I opened it for Karen, they did the same thing, and I made sure to keep it locked from then on."

"We didn't break in," said May, sniffling.

"How did you open it?" Dad demanded.

"She hides the key under the rug in the doll house," said Amy.

"You spies! You'll never come in this room again! Never! I'll never speak to you again!"

"Eve," said Dad. "Please . . . we're about to go on vacation. Amy and May, say you're sorry."

"We're sorry," they said in unison.

"We thought you really wanted to take them with you. We were going to put them in your suitcase as a surprise," said May.

"See," said Mom. "Their intentions weren't so bad."

I couldn't speak. I pressed my lips together and glared at Mom.

Mom turned back to the twins. "You shouldn't have been going through Eve's things without her permission," she said. "You should have asked her. Because accidents can happen."

I couldn't believe it. The twins were not going to be punished. I could just tell. "Mom! Dad!" I yelled. "Are you going to let them get away with this?"

"Nobody's letting anybody get away with

anything," said Dad. "I'm going to order you a new Curly doll right now online. But as soon as I'm finished, we're going to pack the car and get on our way."

"I'm not going!" Hot tears spilled out of my eyes.

"Yes, you are, sweetheart," said Dad. "This is a family vacation. We're going as a family."

I didn't say anything. I knew I didn't have a choice. I couldn't even stay at Aunt Norma's with Lindsay and Karen because they were already on their way to Twin Falls.

"Now, Eve," said Mom. "Dad just said that we'll get you a new doll. And the twins are sorry. Please don't sulk."

"It's not a doll. It's a collectible action figure." I picked up the headless Curly. He looked pathetic.

"It's not fair," I said. "The twins get away with everything."

"Think vacation," said Dad. "Think swimming pool."

The twins peeped out from around Dad's legs. "We really are sorry," said Amy.

"Sorry, Eve," said May, not even mangling the words. It didn't make me any happier.

I ignored them. But if by any chance I ran into a good fairy over the weekend, I was going to ask her to turn them both into goons.

6

DOUBLE DUTCH, DOUBLE TROUBLE

I refused to talk to anybody during the whole drive to Twin Falls. For once, the twins seemed really scared. They didn't poke me or touch me the whole time. Dad kept trying to get everybody to sing songs and play games. He even made the mistake of starting "Little Rabbit Fou-Fou," but one look at my face and even he gave up.

When we finally pulled into the driveway of Twin Falls Resort, Lindsay, Karen, and Aunt Norma were waiting outside for us. There was a big banner over the entrance to the hotel that read "Welcome to Twinsville."

"This place is so cool," said Lindsay. Then she saw my face. "What's wrong?"

"Two guesses!" I said.

"What did the putrid pair do this time?" asked Karen.

"The gruesome twosome broke Curly's head," I said.

"Eve," said Mom. "Try to put that behind you. And please, don't call Amy and May 'the gruesome twosome.' And you, too, Lindsay and Karen. No calling them 'putrid pair' or any other fruit and vegetable names. Remember, you're surrounded by twins and triplets. I think this weekend it might offend people."

Mom was probably right. Everywhere I looked there were pairs of people dressed in identical outfits. When two pairs met, they shrieked and giggled and hugged. There are names for bunches of things: a gaggle of geese, a pride of lions, a crash of rhinos, a blessing of unicorns. What do you call a bunch of twins: a tickle of twins? Whatever the name for it was, it was not a pretty sight.

Mom and Dad took us into the lobby. Aunt Norma showed them where to register before she took Lindsay and Karen off to the pool.

Mom and Dad said I could join them if I kept an eye on the twins while they registered.

We were wandering around the lobby when a familiar voice yelled, "Yoo-hoo! April, isn't it?"

I turned around. It was Mrs. Keller. "Are you talking to me?" I asked.

"Yes, isn't your name April? The older sister of these adorable little munchkins?" She bent down and pinched the twins' cheeks.

"No. My name is Eve," I told her. "But April comes before May—and May's my little sister."

"April showers bring May flowers," chirped May. "I'm May."

Amy had to have her share of the attention. She wasn't used to May speaking up first. "I'm Amy. 'A' is the first letter of the alphabet."

"And aren't you both pretty as flowers and smart as whips," cooed Mrs. Keller.

They both preened.

"I don't know why anyone would think a whip was smart," I muttered.

Mrs. Keller turned to me. "Now, June, be sure to tell your parents to register these little darlings for the talent show. It's the biggest event of the weekend."

Mrs. Keller couldn't seem to look at the twins without calling them little darlings. "My name isn't June. June comes after May—and that's not me. My name's Eve— remember her, the first woman?"

Mrs. Keller looked down at me. "Well, let me give you a program. We have so many activities. You'll be very busy."

I looked at the program she gave me. There was a double Dutch rope-jumping contest, a twin weenie roast, and then of course, the talent contest. I could see that singletons didn't count in this world.

"Oh, look," gushed Mrs. Keller. "There are two of my favorite twins. Harry and Gary's parents have been bringing them to the festival since they were babies." She waved. "Yoo-hoo! Harry! Gary! Come over here."

Two boys came over. They looked about my age. They were dressed in matching outfits—plaid shorts and T-shirts with their names stenciled on them.

"Hi," said May. "We're twins."

I stared at her. Something about being at a twin festival seemed to have made her bolder.

"Us, too. I'm the older brother," said the one with "Harry" on his shirt. "I was born two minutes before this guy. He's *always* two minutes behind."

"Harry and Gary have a magic act, don't you?" said Mrs. Keller. "Why don't you all get acquainted. Lots to do. Must run!"

Harry snickered. "Yeah, I make Gary disappear," he said. Gary didn't say anything.

Amy and May were staring at Gary as if they expected him to disappear then and there.

"We're supposed to meet my aunt at the pool. We gotta go get changed," I said. I took Amy and May by the hand and headed off to find Mom and Dad. I had had enough of the silent Gary and his mean brother, Harry. And more than enough of people like Mrs. Keller who thought twins were the best thing in the world.

The pool was even weirder than the lobby. If the twins in the lobby looked odd, it seemed even odder to see them in bathing suits— baby twins in matching diapers and twins who looked like grandmothers who had identical pieces of skin hanging down from their arms.

Aunt Norma waved. "Isn't this place a hoot?"

"Hurry up, Eve." Lindsay and Karen splashed me with water.

I went to the steps and was about to slip into the water when I heard a voice. "Hey, you pulled a fast one on us. We thought you were a singleton, but you're part of triplets." It was Gary. Or maybe Harry. With their T-shirts off, it was impossible to tell them apart.

I stared at him. "What are you talking about?"

"You and your sisters. Wow! Multiples must really run in your family. One set of triplets and one set of twins. At this festival, that's something to brag about."

"Are you Gary or Harry?" I asked him.

"Gary," he said.

"Well, Gary. I'm glad you found your voice, but how could you think I'm a triplet? My twin sisters are way younger than me. You saw them."

"I didn't mean them," said Gary. He pointed to Karen and Lindsay. "Aren't you three girls triplets?"

Karen, Lindsay, and I stared at each other and giggled. We were all wearing our sunflower bathing suits. Before we could say anything, Gary's twin brother, Harry, was pointing at us and shouting to his mother.

"Hey, Mom, look—here's a family with twins and triplets."

"How fascinating," gushed Harry's mom. I thought she sounded a lot like Mrs. Keller.

"Still," shouted Harry, "twins rule!" He did a cannonball, landing practically right on my head.

I climbed out of the pool to get away from Harry, but his mother wouldn't let me alone. "Imagine. Two sets of multiples in one family. I can't wait to see what you'll do in the talent show."

I rolled my eyes. I was so glad that my

parents didn't think that having twins was the best thing since sliced bread. Hearing twins screeching "Twins rule!" made me want to screech myself.

I got back in the pool and swam over to Lindsay. Karen was sitting by the side of the pool, glancing through the program. "Is anybody besides me a little tired of this 'twins rule' stuff?" I asked.

"I am!" said Lindsay.

"Going through this program is making me nuts," said Karen. "It's all twins this and twins that. Wait—they're having a double Dutch competition right now. And double Dutch takes three people. Two to swing the rope, and one to jump. It can't be open to just twins, can it? Let's go enter."

I pulled myself out of the pool. "Let's go! I love double Dutch."

Amy and May trailed after us. "Where are you going?" Amy asked.

"To the double Dutch contest. You can't come. I'm going with Lindsay and Karen."

"Uh-oh," said Karen.

"Uh-oh, what?" I asked.

"There's a problem. Look." Karen handed me the program.

I read the paragraph underneath the heading "Double Dutch." "For multiples," said the fine print.

"Looks like you'll have to do it with the twins," said Lindsay.

"Oh, goody," said May. "We'll do it good."

"Give them a chance," said Karen.

I really am good at double Dutch. I wanted to win the contest—I had no choice. I looked down at Amy and May. "Okay," I said. "But you've got to keep the ropes moving at the same time."

"We'll do it good," Amy promised.

"All they have to do is to keep turning," said Lindsay.

"We'll help them," said Karen.

When it was our turn, the twins took hold of the ropes. Karen and Lindsay went to help them, but the judges said they had to stand a foot away.

Amy and May giggled. "We do it alone!" they said. "You'll see."

They started turning. I was impressed—

they actually remembered how to swing the ropes so there was a hole big enough for me. I got the rhythm and then jumped in.

I heard a big "Whoops!" come out of Amy.

"Whoops! Whoops!" shouted May.

Then next thing I knew, one rope was whipped around my legs. The other rope got caught around my middle.

"We fix it! We fix it!" shouted Amy and May. They ran in opposite directions around me. The ropes got tighter and tighter! I was being trussed up like a chicken.

"Stop!" I shouted.

The judges and everyone else were laughing. Lindsay and Karen came over to help unravel me.

"This would have made a great comedy routine," said Lindsay.

"Yeah," said Karen. "It looks like something out of a Three Stooges movie. Maybe you three should try out for the talent show."

"Can we, Eve?" asked May.

"We three!" yelled Amy.

"No!" I shouted at them. "There is no such thing as 'we three.' The only three is

me, Lindsay and Karen. Go back to Mom and Dad."

The twins looked crestfallen, but at least they didn't argue with me. There was something to be said for having them feel guilty.

7

CURLY, LARRY, AND MOE

Lindsay, Karen, and I headed back to the pool after the double Dutch fiasco. We ran into Harry and Gary and their mother. "Harry and Gary are about to practice for this evening's talent show," she said. "Are you three entered?"

Lindsay and Karen looked around to see which three she was talking about. The twins had run ahead to Mom and Dad.

"Of course," Mrs. Harry-Gary continued, "even though you have so many multiples in your family, talent counts most. And my Harry and Gary are pretty talented. They won the trophy last year and the year before that with their magic act. What do you girls do?"

"Uh . . . we're not—" Lindsay started to say.

I clapped my hand over Lindsay's mouth. "Don't give our secrets away too quickly," I said.

"Well, I don't know why you need to be so secretive." She huffed away, dragging Harry and Gary after her.

Lindsay stared at me. "Why did you do that?" she asked.

"Because I've got an idea," I said. "In fact, you gave me the idea. How would you like to prove once and for all that you don't have to be a twin to have talent?"

"What do you have in mind?" Karen asked me.

"Let's go up to our room, and I'll tell you."

When we got upstairs I locked the door. I didn't want the twins barging in.

"Okay," said Karen. "Let's hear your idea."

"Remember when you said the twins and I should enter the talent show as the Three Stooges? Well, you know the routines as well as I do. The three of *us* could be the Three Stooges."

"But the talent show is for twins," Lindsay said.

"They might think we're triplets, but let them think what they want to think."

"But we aren't triplets," said Karen. "We aren't even the same age. And we don't look like triplets."

I steered Karen and Lindsay over to the mirror. We looked at ourselves. We were still dressed in our bathing suits. We were all about the same height. We really did look a lot alike. "Harry and Gary and their mother thought we were triplets. They're gaga for all this multiple stuff. And people probably think that we're nonidentical triplets, anyhow. Come on," I said, "let's do it. We'll be Curly, Moe, and Larry. We'll blow Harry and Gary's magic act out of the water."

"I want to go as Curly," said Karen.

"Curly's bald, completely bald," Lindsay reminded her.

"Do you think I should shave my head?" Karen asked.

"Naw," I said. "We'll put a bathing cap over you."

In a beige bathing cap, Karen's head did look bald—so she looked like Curly. Lindsay combed her naturally frizzy hair forward to form a bushy ridge around her head. Now, she looked like Larry.

"I'll be Moe," I said. I combed my hair so it looked like I had cut it with a bowl. I liked playing Moe. Moe is always the boss of the outfit. It's always Moe's schemes that get them in trouble.

We were the Three Stooges!

Someone banged on the door. I opened it a crack. It was the twins. "Go away!" I said.

"Let us in!" screamed Amy.

"What do you want?" I asked through the crack in the door.

"We need help. Mom and Dad said we can enter the talent show," said Amy. "We're gonna sing 'Little Rabbit Fou-Fou.'"

"So go bop each other on the head," I said. "We're busy."

"Please, Eve," whined Amy.

"No," I said, starting to close the door.

"Pretty please, Eve," begged Amy. She

started singing "Little Rabbit Fou-Fou."

May started in a half beat behind her and on a completely different note.

Karen rolled her eyes.

I closed the door on them. I couldn't believe they expected me to help them after what they did to Curly. And after they tied me up with ropes. This time, they weren't going to get their own way.

Karen, Lindsay, and I chose a scene from *Mutts to You*, one of my favorite Three Stooges movies. It is one of the funniest movies in the world. The Three Stooges work in a dog laundry, and they mistake a baby for a dog. We practiced the part when Moe tries to slap Curly and hits Larry instead. Then we pulled each other's noses the way the Stooges do.

We worked all afternoon getting our routine down pat. Maybe we'd fall flat on our faces. But so what! If you're the Three Stooges, falling on your faces is always part of the act.

There was banging on the door. The twins again.

"Let us in!" screamed Amy.

"What's wrong?" I asked.

"We want you to hear us."

I knew they would never go away so I let them in. "One verse," I warned.

They started to sing. Karen's eyes widened. They sounded even *verse* than usual.

"Maybe they give out a prize for stopping singing," said Karen. "That way, you might win."

The twins looked at her. They kind of guessed they were being insulted, but they weren't quite sure.

"You sound like night-mare-gales." I wanted to get them out of our room so we could rehearse one more time. I had really meant to say 'nightingales,' but it had come out as 'night-mare-gales.'

"Is a night-mare-gale good?" Amy asked.

"Oh, yeah." I shooed them out of the room.

8

OWATAGOOSIAM

When it was time for the show to start, Lindsay, Karen, and I went downstairs. We found the talent coordinator, who was scheduling the acts. I took an application and looked at it carefully. I couldn't believe our good luck. It just asked for the names of family members who were entered. It didn't say "for multiples only" or anything like that. We weren't even cheating.

I filled out the application and gave it to the coordinator. She smiled at us. "You know, we've had so many triplets over the years, and you are the first ones to think of coming as the Three Stooges. Good luck, girls!"

We went to the backstage area of the performance tent. There were a lot of twins dressed up as munchkins from *The Wizard of Oz*. There were tap-dancing twins, middle-aged twins dressed as babies, and twin babies dressed like grown-ups.

We saw Harry dressed up in a magician's outfit. His brother, Gary, looked nervous. He was biting his fingernails. The coordinator came up to them. "You're on now," she said.

"Out of my way!" Harry pushed me aside with his magic wand. "It's time for the star of the show to go on."

Lindsay, Karen, and I stood backstage and watched their act.

Harry strode out onstage first, wrapping his cloak dramatically around him. "I'm Harry the Great! Named for the Great Harry Houdini himself. I'd like to introduce my not-so-great assistant, Gary, the doofus. He's my younger brother by two minutes. I will now put my brother into a trance. Gary, repeat after me. 'Owa.'"

"Owa . . ." Gary said.

"Tagoo . . ." said Harry.

"Tagoo," repeated Gary.

"Siam," said Harry.

I rolled my eyes. This was one of the oldest jokes in the world. We had played it on each other in kindergarten.

"Say it faster," commanded Harry.

"Owa . . . tagoo . . . siam," said Gary.

"Again!"

"Owatagoosiam. Owatagoosiam."

The audience finally caught on that Gary was saying, "Oh, what a goose I am." And Harry was making a goose out of his brother all right. All of Harry's magic tricks seemed designed to make Gary look stupid.

For his grand finale, Harry said he would make his brother disappear. First, he made Gary stand inside a booth that had been set up on the stage. He pulled the curtain across the opening. Then Harry went behind the booth. After a few seconds, the curtain opened to reveal one twin dressed in a black cape.

I knew immediately that all they had done was change places. Harry had given Gary his cape. But Gary looked so awkward and nervous that the cape fell off. Now,

maybe if this hadn't been a twin convention, the trick would have worked. I smiled to myself. I wondered if Mrs. Keller thought they were so great now. But I have to admit, the audience seemed to like them. They got a big round of applause.

Backstage, Harry was furious. "You ruined it!" he yelled at Gary. "You were supposed to wrap your cape dramatically, the way I did. Then the audience would have thought I had really made you disappear."

"Harry," I said, "at a twin festival almost everybody can change places."

"Who asked you?" muttered Harry. He pushed me aside. I was even happier than ever that we had decided to enter the talent show—we were sure to beat horrible Harry.

The next act was a tap-dancing duo. They were good, but the audience didn't give them half the applause that Gary and Harry had gotten. I guess there was no accounting for taste at a twin festival.

Amy and May were on in a few minutes. *"Little Rabbit Fou-Fou,"* practiced Amy— off-key, of course.

"Bopped on the head!" screeched May. She grinned up at me. "You said we sing like night-mare-gales."

Harry came bustling by again, still yelling at Gary. "I don't know how you could be so stupid!" he shouted. "Unless they left the brains out during those two minutes you were left behind."

I couldn't believe how obnoxious he was to Gary, just because he was a few minutes older.

"Okay, girls, you're on," said the talent coordinator to Amy and May. She shooed them onstage.

Amy and May took center stage. They screeched out the first notes of the song in the worst off-key voices you could ever hear. *"Little Rabbit Fou-Fou!"*

At first, the audience seemed to think that Amy and May had meant to sing horribly. But the louder they sang, the clearer it became that the twins were trying to really sing. I heard loud giggling from the audience. All the kids were snickering. The adults looked embarrassed.

Just then, Amy and May hit a particularly

bad note. The snickering got louder. Amy and May both looked into the wings to where I was standing. They looked a little sick to their stomachs. I could tell they knew the audience was laughing *at* them. They were dying out there—and it wasn't fun to watch.

I started to get a sick feeling in my own stomach. Amy and May had asked for help, and I had ignored them. Was I just as bad as Harry?

I grabbed Lindsay and Karen. "Come on."

9

THE THREE STOOGES TO THE RESCUE

The lights onstage were blinding. It took a few seconds for our eyes to adjust. Amy and May had stopped singing.

I went up to the microphone. Lindsay and Karen stood next to me. I pulled the twins in front of us.

"Ladies and gentlemen," I said. "The Three Stooges are here to help the Little Rabbits Fou-Fou. We are family!"

Everyone started laughing and hooting. All you have to do is mention the Three Stooges and people crack up. We got a round of applause just for our names.

I continued in a loud voice, "The Three

Stooges plus Two Little Stooges will now teach all of you the famous song, 'Little Rabbit Fou-Fou!'"

Lindsay, Karen, and I sang out, *"Little Rabbit Fou-Fou, hopping through the forest . . . came upon a field mouse, bopped it on the head."* Karen's voice was beautiful, and it rang out across the room.

When we got to the bopping part, the twins were perfect pretending they were bopped. With our voices, especially Karen's, carrying the tune, we had the audience laughing and singing with us—not at us.

Each time we got to the end of the verse, Karen, Lindsay, and I sang into the microphone. *"Little Rabbit Fou-Fou, stop bopping field mice, or I'll turn you into a goon!"*

Finally, the last field mouse got bopped on the head. I shouted into the microphone. "The moral of the story . . ." I paused the way all good comics learn to pause.

"HARE TODAY—GOON TOMORROW!" I shouted.

"Nyuk, nyuk, nyuk!" We all joined hands

and did Curly's laugh. The audience cracked up. Then we pulled each other's noses the way the Three Stooges always did.

We got a huge round of applause. I pumped my arm in the air. I knew we had scored big. I loved it. Everybody loved us, and I loved making everybody laugh. The twins singing off-key had just made our act together funnier.

We ran backstage. "'Little Rabbit Fou-Fou' is such a stupid song," hissed a voice. It was Harry.

"Not the way the Three Stooges and Two Little Stooges do it," I said.

"Well, dear, I suppose it's easy to impress the judges when you've got both triplets and twins," said Harry's mother in a sweet tone. I could tell she was annoyed. She knew we were bound to break her darling sons' winning streak.

After the final act, there was a wait and then the judges came onstage. "Ladies and gentlemen," announced the coordinator. "We have a winner. Today was clearly a day for comedy. The winners are the Three Stooges and their little sisters singing a song none of us will ever forget—'Little Rabbit Fou-Fou.' It's amazing—five multiples in one family. One set of triplets and one set of twins."

Uh-oh. I had conveniently forgotten that we weren't exactly one set of triplets and one set of twins.

The coordinator put the trophy in my hand. Naturally, Amy and May hated that I had something they didn't have.

"Hey!" shouted Amy, jumping up and down. "Gimme!"

"Me! Me!" yelped May. She jumped to try to reach the trophy, too.

I held the trophy over their heads. The judges laughed.

"That's ours!" squawked Amy. "We won! We're the twins."

I tried to ignore them.

"We're twins!" said May. Then she pointed at me, Lindsay, and Karen. "They're not! They're simpletons!"

The judges gasped. This was bad. The audience started rumbling. It didn't sound friendly.

10

WE ARE FAMILY!

The whole place was in an uproar. Harry's mother charged the stage, followed by Harry and Gary.

"What exactly is going on?" asked one of the judges.

Harry's mother pointed at us. "Fraud!" she screeched. "You heard them. They're not triplets."

"Is that true?" asked the judge.

"It's absolutely true." Mrs. Keller appeared onstage. She pointed at me. "She's a singleton!"

"Well?" the judge asked. She was looking

right at me, as if she knew I was the ringleader.

"Uh . . . kind of," I stammered. "But . . . but . . ."

Mrs. Keller interrupted my stammering. "This is so against the rules. This is big trouble in Twinsville."

Harry's mother was staring at us like we had turned into cockroaches. "The prize should go to the runners-up—my boys."

"But the talent show entry form doesn't say anything about being twins . . ." I tried to argue.

"Of course not!" yelled Mrs. Keller. "It's open to triplets and other multiples—which you clearly pretended to be."

"Wait just one minute!" Mom came running up onstage.

"Your children perpetrated a fraud!" said Mrs. Keller.

Mom put her hands on her hips. "My daughter is not a fraud. I just looked at the program. The entry form for the talent show clearly asks for the names of family members."

"That's what I saw, Mom," I said.

Dad grinned. "I always said you'll make a great lawyer one day, Eve, just like your mom."

Karen took off her bathing cap. "I'm not even a sister of a twin," she said. "But we're part of the same family."

Lindsay took her hand. "Yeah, we're all cousins."

Harry snatched the trophy from me. "Did you hear that? They're just cousins. I won— I should get the trophy."

"Not so fast," said Mom, turning to the coordinator. "Once again, I must point out that the entry form asks for the names of family members only. Well, they *are* from the same family—the twins, my nieces, and my wonderful daughter, Eve. You don't have to be a twin to be special."

"Way to go, Mom." I was so happy Mom was sticking up for me like that.

Mom turned to the judges. "Nobody's taking that trophy away from anybody," she said. She sounded polite but you knew she meant business.

The judges whispered among themselves,

frantically looking at the program. At last, the coordinator went to the microphone. "Ladies and gentlemen, boys and girls, may we have your attention. As we said before, we do have a winner—five winners from a very special family." She yanked the trophy away from Harry and gave it back to me.

Lindsay and Karen picked Amy and May up. We all held the trophy high! Everyone cheered.

Unfortunately, I never got a good look at the trophy until we were in the car on our way home.

"Hey!" piped up Amy. "That looks like me!"

"No, me!" said May.

I looked down at the trophy in my lap. I couldn't believe it. The twins were right. The handles of the trophy were two little girls with long hair and identical features.

"Let's win it again next year!" said Amy.

"Yeah!" shouted May.

They started screeching in my ears. *"Little Rabbit Fou-Fou . . ."*

"Mom, Dad!" I yelled. "Make them stop."

"Fou-fou–fa—fa . . ." shouted Amy off-key.

"Fou-fou fala-fala." May joined in.

They poked at me. Their fingers were sticky and bright orange because they'd been eating cheese doodles.

I sank down in my seat. The big trouble in little Twinsville was coming home with me. If only we could have left one of them there.

Like I said, two was a very big mistake. I only ordered one.